Kaiden sure missed his Friends

Written by:
Takiya Jackson

Mynd Matters Publishing
715 Peachtree Street NE
Suites 100 & 200
Atlanta, GA 30308

978-1-953307-70-5 (pbk)
978-1-953307-69-9 (hdcv)

DEDICATION

To Kaiden,
Living through a global pandemic was difficult.
Not seeing friends from school was challenging.
But you did it.

Stay resilient!
-Mom

"Good morning, mom. What will I wear to school today?" Kaiden asked.
"Oh honey, you don't have in-person school today, remember?" Mom explained.
"What's in-person school?" asked Kaiden.
"It's school where you actually go into the building. Things have changed and you have to stay home for school for a while," replied Mom.
Sad and confused, Kaiden sighed.
"I sure miss my friends."

"Let's sit down and chat for a minute. You're super smart and old enough for us to talk about some of the things happening around us. Right now our country and the world are going through something called a pandemic. Can you say that word, Kaiden?"

"Pandemic," Kaiden said. "Wait! What's a pandemic?"

Mom laughed. "I'm getting there, sir. Calm down!

A pandemic is when a lot of people get really sick from the same illness and it spreads across several countries. Right now, lots of people are catching-"
"Covid-19!" Kaiden exclaimed, finishing his mom's sentence.
"Exactly! The virus is called Covid-19 or Coronavirus and because so many people are catching this disease, schools have decided to have you all stay home for a while."
Kaiden nodded his head and sighed. "I understand mama, but I sure miss my friends."

For the next few months, Kaiden logged in to school on his computer. He wasn't able to visit friends at their houses or go to fun places to jump around anymore. However, he found new ways to stay connected! He learned to video call his friends and family and was able to play live games with friends on his game system.

Although these things were fun, he sure missed his friends.

make it happen

12

"Kaiden wake up!" Mom said excitedly. (Sleepy Kaiden wakes up)
"Yes, Mom? What is it?" asked Kaiden.
"You're going back to school today!" exclaimed Mom. "But remember, things will look a little different now."
Kaiden looks confused, "I forgot, he shrugs. How will it be different?"
"Well for one thing you have to be sure to keep your mask on at all times and others should too," said Mom.
"Ok" he says.
"You have to make sure you're washing your hands and not touching your mouth or eyes," said Mom.
"Yes ma'am," said Kaiden.
"No hugging or touching your friends or teachers," said Mom.
"Whatttt!" Kaiden exclaimed. "But I always give Ms. Williams a hug when I go into class."
"I know baby, but for your safety and hers that can't happen anymore. But don't worry, you will see all your friends today and I know they're excited!"

Kaiden had butterflies. Although he didn't know what to expect, he was excited and just wished things would just go back to normal. It had been so long since he had seen everyone.

He sure missed his friends.

"We're here!" Mom shouted excitedly.

"Welllll, aren't you going to walk me in?" Kaiden asked.

"Not this time, bud. That's one of those changes we talked about. Parents and visitors are not allowed in the building to help keep icky yucky germs away. Plus, you're a big boy now. You can do it, go ahead. I will be here when you get out of school later."

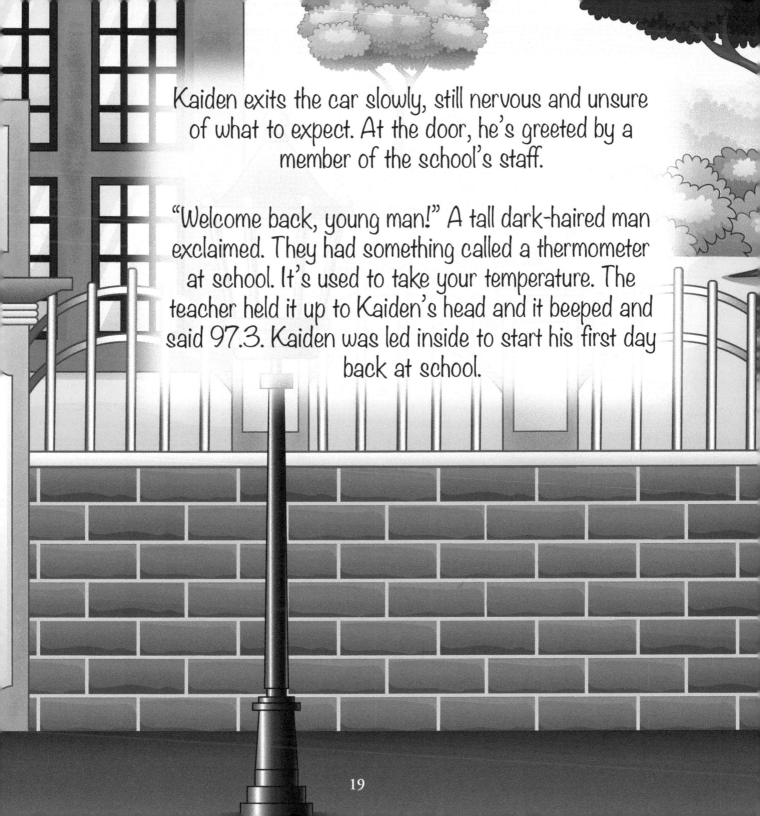

Kaiden exits the car slowly, still nervous and unsure of what to expect. At the door, he's greeted by a member of the school's staff.

"Welcome back, young man!" A tall dark-haired man exclaimed. They had something called a thermometer at school. It's used to take your temperature. The teacher held it up to Kaiden's head and it beeped and said 97.3. Kaiden was led inside to start his first day back at school.

"Kaiden! Is that you?" Jeremiah, one of Kaiden's classmates from last year, said through his mask as he walked over.

"Hey, Jeremiah! Yes, it's me!"

Kaiden and Jeremiah head to their classroom where they see Ms. Williams jumping up and down with excitement and waving at them.

"Welcome back boys! How are you both? I have missed you soooo much!" she exclaimed.

Kaiden looked at Jeremiah and then back at Ms. Williams and knew he was going to have a GREAT first day back.

He sure had missed his friends.

ABOUT THE AUTHOR

Takiya Jackson, educator and mother, received her Bachelor of Science in Psychology from Georgia State University. With a concentration in Early Childhood Development, she used her knowledge to transition into a career in Education.

She is a mom to her son, Kaiden, and two fur babies, Nala and Zoe.

Kaiden Sure Missed His Friends was inspired by the challenges Kaiden and other students faced during the Covid-19 pandemic.

"The constant from my son was always, "I miss my friends.""

CPSIA information can be obtained
at www.ICGtesting.com
Printed in the USA
BVHW021701230621
610223BV00013B/689

9 781953 307705